Names: Plum Coconut, author. | Marzi, Emilia, illustrator.
Title: Poopasaurus / by Plum Coconut; illustrated by Emilia Marzi.
Description: Logan, UT: Plum Coconut, 2022.
Summary: Poopasaurus is a toddler Tyrannosaurus rex who becomes potty trained.
Identifiers: LCCN: 2022919144 | 978-1-955591-03-4 (paperback)
| 978-1-955591-04-1 (board) | 978-1-955591-05-8 (ebook)
Subjects: LCSH Dinosaurs--Juvenile fiction. | Toilet training--Juvenile fiction. | BISAC JUVENILE FICTION /
Animals / Dinosaurs & Prehistoric Creatures | JUVENILE FICTION / Health & Daily Living / Toilet Training
Classification: LCC PZ7.1 .P628 Po 2022 | DDC [E]--dc23

POOPASAURUS

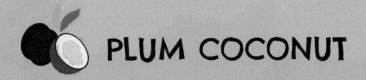

PLUM COCONUT

ILLUSTRATIONS: Emilia Marzi

Poopasaurus Rex – it's no fun
to have a wet poopy diaper.

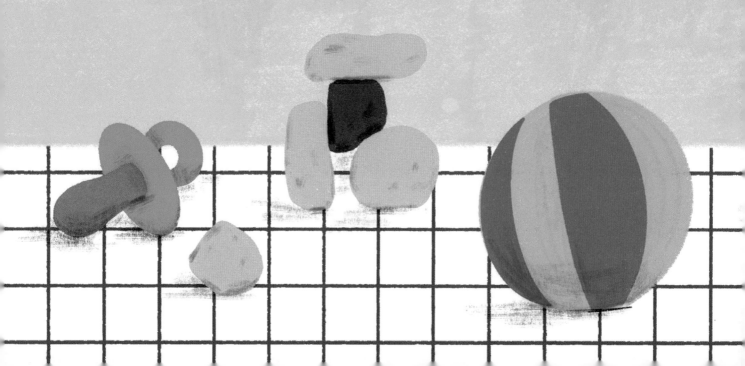

And Mamasaurus and Dadasaurus don't want to change poopy diapers forever.

It's time for you to say
goodbye to those diapers.
Diapers are for babies.
You are now a big dinosaur!

It's time to use the potty.

Your mommy and daddy use their toilet every day.

Poopasaurus - you should try to pee
and poop on your big Dino potty too!

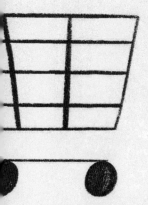

Your potty is special.
Mamasaurus and Dadasaurus
got it just for you.

Be patient Poopasaurus and don't give up! Going on your potty is new and will take practice.

One day soon
you will pee
and poop
on your potty!

Then you can learn to wipe
yourself clean.

And wash and dry your hands.

Mamasaurus and Dadasaurus
will be so proud.

You can put those old diapers
in the trash.

And put on your big Dino underwear!

Great job
Poopasaurus!

THE END

DOWNLOAD A
FREE
POTTY CHART!

Point your phone camera
at the QR code and click
the link it gives you!

www.plumcoconut.com/pc